First published in Switzerland under the title *Gustav Ganz Gross.*

First published in the United States, Great Britain, Canada, Australia, and New Zealand in 2015 by NorthSouth Books, Inc., an imprint of NordSüd Verlag AG, CH-8005 Zürich, Switzerland.

Distributed in the United States by NorthSouth Books, Inc., New York 10016.
Library of Congress Cataloging-in-Publication Data is available.
ISBN: 978-0-7358-4242-7 (trade edition)
1 3 5 7 9 • 10 8 6 4 2
Printed in Germany by Grafisches Centrum Cuno GmbH & Co. KG, Calbe, June 2015.

www.northsouth.com

Hans de Beer

Nugget ON TOP OF THE World

North
South

In the big city there lived a little dachshund whose name was Nugget. In two months he would be one year old.

Nugget had nice owners and a soft bed. There was just one problem—a BIG problem. Nugget thought he was far too small.

Everything in his house was bigger than he was. He could never see anything that happened higher than the tip of his nose.

But being small had its advantages. Nugget had no difficulty getting through the cat flap in the kitchen door.

Even as a young pup he learned to cross the street when the light was green. So now he was allowed to walk as often as he liked in the park around the corner—all by himself!

But Nugget had the same problem in the park as he did at home. Everything was much bigger and taller than he was. He could only look at things from underneath, and so he never had a really good view of anything. He felt as if he was getting smaller and smaller.

Nugget had lots of friends, but, of course, he was the smallest of them all. Nugget was tired of not being able to see everything.

His best friend, Emma, knew just what to do to help. Emma's good friend was a huge Great Dane, and so they put Nugget on his back. But even from up there Nugget couldn't see anything. That's because he was frightened.

"Let me down!" he cried, his voice trembling with fear.

Outside the shop around the corner, Nugget stood and dreamed as he looked at the television screens. Nugget would love to be able to see a view like that in the real world!

"If you want a great view, go to the big bridge that crosses the river," Emma said to the little dachshund. "It's not far from here and is very easy to find. Because at the foot of the bridge is the fish market. So you just have to follow your nose."

The next morning Emma pointed Nugget in the direction of the bridge.

"But you must come back before dark," she said. "Because at night the city looks very different than during the day."

"I promise," said Nugget confidently, and away he went.

The closer he got to the river, the taller the buildings became. He could see less and less of the sky. But the smell of fish grew stronger and stronger, so Nugget trotted happily onward.

"What's a little dachshund like you doing in a big city like this?" laughed a big tomcat.

"I've come from the park, and I'm on my way to the fish market, Mr. Tomcat," said Nugget politely.

"Ah, I often go to the fish market," said the cat. "It's not far away—you'll soon be there. But make sure you get home before dark, little dachshund."

Nugget wasn't listening anymore. When he turned the corner, he saw the fish market, and behind that the huge bridge. Nugget was very excited.

HB-11-14

11,–
9,25
7,50
7,50

In the market everything smelled strongly of fish. Nugget saw a mother with her child.

"Up, up! Me see too!" begged the little boy. The mother lifted him up and showed him the fish and then set him down again. "Up, up!" demanded the boy.

"Be patient," said the mother, laughing. "When you're bigger, you can look for as long as you like."

The thought of growing bigger was music to Nugget's ears.

Cheerfully Nugget began to climb the steps that led to the bridge. Step by step, higher and higher. Nugget was already out of breath. But he bravely continued.

At long last he reached the top.

It was even more beautiful than he had imagined. Below him flowed a wide river. On all sides he could see sky and water. He could even look down on some of the tall buildings. Nugget was delighted and fascinated by the wonderful view. His little nose was firmly pressed against the railing.

"So this is what it's like to be big!" he said happily.

Nugget had never been this high up before. He simply couldn't stop looking.

Slowly the sun sank below the horizon, and the sky glowed with color.

"It's even more beautiful than on television!" sighed Nugget.

TELEVISION! Suddenly he thought of home. It was already getting dark, and drops of rain were falling from the clouds. He had to get home before nightfall.

He started to run as fast as his little legs could carry him—down from the bridge and then through the market in the pouring rain.

But Nugget had waited too long. It was getting darker and darker. And now everything looked different. How could Nugget find his way back to the park? He found himself standing at the same corner for the third time. His soft, warm bed seemed impossibly far away.

"So you've lost your way, have you, little dachshund?" a voice said suddenly in the dark. It was the big tomcat. "My name is Sam. You'd better come with me. I'll take you back to the park, my little friend."

"Thank you very much, Mr. Sam," said Nugget, extremely relieved.

Sam had no trouble finding his way through the dark streets. Soon they reached the park, and a few moments later Nugget slipped joyfully through the cat flap.

His owners had been worried about him, but now they gave him some especially yummy food. They even let him up on the sofa!

Nugget thought, *Being small is not such a big problem after all.*

"I'll simply wait and grow a bit bigger," he decided. Then he curled up happily for the night. "Tomorrow, I'll tell Emma how beautiful it was on the bridge!"